Movie Storybook

Based on the motion picture from
Walt Disney Pictures and Steven Spielberg

Executive Producers
STEVEN SPIELBERG   KATHLEEN KENNEDY   FRANK MARSHALL
Produced by
ROBERT WATTS
Screenplay by
JEFFREY PRICE & PETER SEAMAN
Directed by
ROBERT ZEMECKIS
Storybook adapted by
JUSTINE KORMAN

A GOLDEN BOOK • NEW YORK
Western Publishing Company, Inc., Racine, Wisconsin 53404

Maroon Cartoon Studio was a busy place where cartoons were made. The people and animals who starred in the cartoons were called Toons, and they lived and worked in Toontown.

Toons could do all the funny things you see in cartoons. They could walk through walls, float in a giant soap bubble, or get squashed flat by a steamroller and then spring to life again. Toons worked hard at making people laugh.

Inside the studio a Toon named Roger Rabbit was struggling to get his scene right.

"Stars!" Roger's director yelled at the tweeting birds circling the rabbit's head. "The script calls for stars. Let's take it from the top."

A second later a cartoon refrigerator fell on Roger's head once more. Offstage, the studio boss, R. K. Maroon, watched the scene and whispered to a private detective.

"Something is rotten in Toontown," Maroon declared, "and I want you to find out what it is."

Eddie Valiant nodded. As far as he was concerned, the whole silly business of Toontown was rotten. He didn't like cartoons or Toons, but a job was a job.

Maroon told Eddie Valiant to follow a man named Marvin. Marvin was the genius behind the Gag Factory, which supplied funny novelties and props to the cartoon industry.

That night Marvin went to the Ink and Paint Club, a classy café where Toons often performed. Eddie watched Marvin walk through the club, slapping a back here, cracking a joke there, spreading laughter wherever he went. All the Toons loved Marvin, and Marvin loved them.

A waiter presented Marvin with a check to be signed. He
pulled a pen from his pocket with a mischievous wink.

"Oops!" Marvin exclaimed as ink squirted across to the next
table—and all over Eddie's shirt. Marvin burst out laughing.

"Very funny," Valiant snapped sourly. "I'll laugh all the way
to the dry cleaner."

"Calm down, sonny. It's disappearing ink," Marvin said.
"One of my best sellers."

Eddie looked down, and his shirt was perfectly clean.

"No hard feelings, I hope," Marvin said, pressing Eddie's
hand with a hearty shake, which was made heartier still by the
hand buzzer in Marvin's hand.

Eddie's arm was still tingling when the lights went down. A hush of anticipation spread through the crowd. "Jessica!" Valiant heard someone whisper. "It's her!"

And then the most beautiful Toon that Eddie had ever seen glided onstage, wearing a red dress and a smile no one could resist.

"That's Roger Rabbit's sweetheart," Marvin whispered.

Valiant could hardly believe his ears. "What would a beautiful Toon like Jessica see in a funny little rabbit?" he wondered. Then she started to sing, and Eddie forgot everything.

Jessica's act ended, and the audience applauded wildly. After the show, Eddie Valiant followed Marvin backstage and saw him go into Jessica's dressing room. Eddie snapped a photograph of the two of them together through the back window. Then the club's bouncer saw him and threw him into the street.

The next day R. K. Maroon showed Eddie's picture of Jessica and Marvin to Roger Rabbit. Roger got so angry that steam came out of his ears. He burst through the window of R.K.'s office.

Valiant and Maroon peeked through the rabbit-shaped hole.

"I think he's jealous," Eddie said.

But Roger was more hurt than jealous—and not from crashing through the window, either.

"I'm a rabbit," he told himself miserably, "a scaredy-cat, a chicken." Roger thought that Jessica didn't like him anymore because he wasn't a brave, strong hero.

The next morning the police came to Valiant's office.

"Heard the latest?" Lieutenant Santino asked Eddie. "Marvin was killed last night. It looks like your photograph pushed Roger Rabbit too far. We tried to question him, but he ran away."

Eddie scratched his head and tried to figure things out. Was funny little Roger Rabbit a killer? It didn't seem possible. And was it Eddie's fault for taking that picture?

After Santino left, Eddie looked at the picture with his magnifying glass, and he saw something he hadn't noticed before. A piece of paper was sticking out of Marvin's pocket. Written on it were the words *Last Will and Testament*.

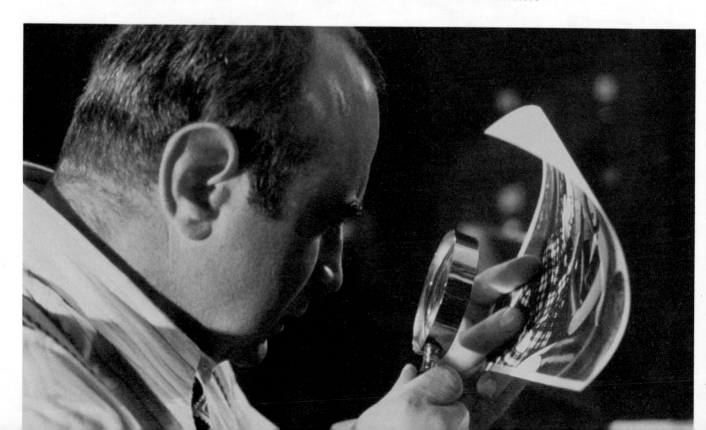

"Now, why would Marvin be carrying around his will?"
Eddie wondered with a yawn. He pulled the folding bed down
from the wall to take a quick nap.

"Aaah!" Eddie exclaimed in surprise as Roger Rabbit
popped out.

"Aaah!" Roger Rabbit shrieked.

"What are you doing here?" Eddie demanded.

"Sleeping," Roger jokingly replied, but one look at Eddie's
angry face made him quickly add, "I'm innocent."

"Then why did you run away?" Valiant asked.

"I'm a rabbit," Roger explained.

"Run away from here," Eddie commanded, chasing him to
the door.

As soon as Eddie turned around, Roger slipped back in through the mail slot. When Valiant opened the closet, Roger was there wearing the detective's coat and hat.

"You've got to help me!" Roger began. "Sure, I was jealous of Marvin and Jessica. I don't blame her for liking a braver guy than me, but I couldn't hurt Marvin. I couldn't hurt a fly. I'm afraid of flies! Besides, Marvin was a good friend to me and to all the Toons. And no matter what happens, I'll always love Jessica. See? Here's a note I wrote her when I visited her dressing room late last night. No one was there, but I found this blank piece of paper. I just had to write down how I feel about her."

Roger showed Eddie the note, but he brushed it aside. Roger put it back in his pocket.

Sirens wailed in the street. Roger's knees buckled together and his ears quivered with fear.

"It's the Toon Patrol!" he exclaimed.

Eddie peeked out the window at the comical weasels of the Toon Patrol piling out of their car.

"Please!" Roger begged. "I'm not brave like you."

Valiant was flattered. But his answer still would have been no, if Roger hadn't clamped a pair of handcuffs on his wrist and Eddie's. Now wherever Roger went Eddie was sure to go—and Eddie didn't feel like going to jail.

Eddie hid Roger and
shouted at the weasels
through the door. "If you're
looking for a rabbit, try a
carrot patch."

Once they'd gone, Eddie
shoved Roger under his
coat and went to the
Terminal Café. His friend
Dolores worked there as a
waitress, and she would
help them.

Dolores brought Eddie and Roger to a back room at the
café. She gave Eddie a hacksaw, and he started sawing to get
the handcuffs off. He was so busy sawing, he didn't see Roger
slip his hand right out of the cuffs.

"Do you mean you could have escaped from the cuffs
anytime?" Eddie asked when he saw Roger was free.

"Of course," said Roger. "I just wanted to make sure you
would help."

Eddie told Roger to stay in the back room while he went to the Ink and Paint Club. Marvin's will might still be in Jessica's dressing room. It was the only clue he had.

Eddie slipped into Jessica's dressing room, but he was immediately knocked out. He awoke to see Judge Doom, the powerful judge of all Toontown, looming above him.

"Looking for something?" hissed the judge. Jessica was sitting next to Eddie. He wondered what she had to do with the dreaded Doom.

"Where's Marvin's will?" Doom demanded. "I want it!"

Eddie insisted he didn't know. Doom searched Eddie's pockets and questioned him until Eddie convinced him he didn't have the will.

"That will must be more important than I thought," Eddie said to himself.

When Eddie got back to the café, he found Roger singing, telling jokes to the customers, and smashing plates on his head. Valiant grabbed Roger and dragged him to the back room.

"You're supposed to be hiding here," Valiant snapped. "Doom could be here any minute."

Valiant was right. Doom burst into the café, followed by his weasels. Eddie guessed they had followed him there.

Eddie and Roger watched Doom through a peephole in the door.

"I'm looking for Roger Rabbit," Doom announced. "There is a $10,000 reward."

Eddie felt sorry for Roger. He had trusted the Terminal regulars. Now one would probably turn him in for the money.

Sure enough Angelo, the cab driver, spoke up. "White fur? Long ears? Makes people laugh?"

"That's the one!" Doom shouted.

"I've seen him," Angelo said. "In the movies!"

Everyone but Doom burst out laughing. Even his weasels laughed.

Then Doom noticed the record on the Terminal's record player. It was "I'm Just Wild About Lettuce," Roger's theme song. "That rabbit is here, I know it," Doom said. "Get the Dip."

The Dip was a terrible liquid that could dissolve Toons and make them disappear for good.

Doom began tapping a rhythm on the walls, counter, and tables with his knuckles. "Da da-da daaa-dum..." it went, over and over.

Roger was entranced by the rhythm. It was irresistible to all Toons.

"Shave and a haircut..." Doom shouted.

Roger couldn't help himself. He burst out of the back room and shouted the conclusion of the jingle: "Two bits."

The weasels burst out laughing, and Eddie decided it was
time to make his move. He grabbed Roger and ran out of the
café. Outside, a friendly voice asked, "Where to?" It was
Benny, a Toon taxi. Eddie and Roger jumped in as the weasels
poured out of the café.

"Eddie," Roger said, "meet Benny the Cab." Benny sped
down the street and dropped them off at a movie theater where
Eddie and Roger hid in the dark. Dolores joined them soon
after.

"Let me borrow your car, Dolores," Eddie said. "You keep
an eye on the rabbit while I pay a visit to R. K. Maroon. I
think he knows a lot more than he told me." Eddie dashed out
of the theater.

When Dolores wasn't looking, Roger ran out. "I'm going to
help Eddie. This is my big chance to be brave," Roger thought.

Unknown to Eddie, Roger followed the detective to Maroon Cartoon Studio. He saw Eddie walk toward R. K. Maroon's office, but being a timid rabbit, Roger decided to wait in an alley outside.

Eddie found R. K. Maroon in the office. Maroon pulled out a gun, but Eddie quickly squirted him with a blast from a seltzer bottle. Eddie grabbed the gun. "Now talk," he said.

"Cloverleaf Company was trying to buy my studio and Marvin's Gag Factory. They wouldn't take my place without his," Maroon explained.

"Cloverleaf," Eddie said. "Isn't that the company that just bought the Red Car Trolley Company?"

"Yes," Maroon said. "That's part of the plan. I didn't realize, when I agreed to sell, that it would mean the end of Toontown. That's why Marvin refused to sell. Now, unless his will is found before midnight, Toontown will be—"

Suddenly sirens pierced the night. "It's the Toon Patrol," Maroon exclaimed. Then he was gone.

Out in the alley, Roger was checking out Eddie's car. Suddenly someone hit him over the head. Then that someone stuffed the helpless rabbit into the trunk of a big fancy car.

Inside, Eddie waited for his chance to escape. His mind was filled with questions. "Who is Cloverleaf? Why does the company want to destroy Toontown? And where is Marvin's will?" he wondered.

Valiant ran from the studio and jumped into his car.
Just then the big fancy car screeched out of the parking lot.
Eddie followed it, wondering who else had come to the studio
that night and why. The car was heading straight for Toontown.

The big car whizzed down dark streets and through tunnels. It finally stopped in front of the Gag Factory. Jessica was driving! Eddie grabbed her as she stepped out of the car.

"Now it's time to do some singing. What are you doing?" Eddie demanded.

"I'm just trying to help Roger. Doom is determined to Dip him. I was hoping to find Marvin's will, or at least something to help clear Roger," Jessica explained.

"Then I owe you an apology," Eddie said. "We might as well work together, as long as we're on the same side."

Roger silently slipped out of the trunk of Jessica's car. He
was still hoping for a chance to be a hero. Suddenly, before
Roger could shout a warning, Jessica and Eddie were
surrounded by weasels. Roger quickly jumped into a dumpster
to avoid being captured himself.

Roger shivered when he recognized the voice of Doom
ordering his weasels to tie up Jessica and Eddie. The prisoners
were taken inside the factory.

"How nice to have a captive audience to help me celebrate
my victory over Toontown," the judge cackled.

"What are you talking about?" Eddie asked.

"This!" Doom said, pointing to a huge blue velvet drape. He
pulled a cord and the curtain dropped to reveal a big vehicle
with spray guns.

"This is my Dipmobile! With it I can erase Toontown
forever!"

"You're crazy," Eddie declared.

"Perhaps, but who is tied up and helpless?" Doom replied.

"Why erase Toontown?" Eddie argued. "What can you gain?"

"A freeway," Doom said. Then Doom explained his evil plan. "I own Cloverleaf Company. I bought Red Car Trolley Company so I could close it down. Then there will be no public transportation. People will have to drive cars. People will be driving on this freeway night and day. They'll need gas stations, restaurants, tire stores, car dealers, and I'll own them all. Soon Toontown will be mine, and I will destroy it to build eight lanes of shimmering cement—a freeway."

"Not if I can help it," Roger Rabbit declared as he burst out of a drainage grate in the floor.

"Let them go," he demanded.

Jessica cooed, "Oh, Roger! You're so brave."

Roger's furry chest swelled with pride. "The only thing that can stop me now," he said, "is a ton of bricks."

Doom smiled as he flicked a switch. Suddenly a ton of cartoon bricks came crashing down on poor Roger. Stars danced in dizzy circles around the rabbit's head. The weasels laughed so hard, they nearly fainted.

"Silence, fools," Doom commanded.

The weasels snickered as they tied Roger and Jessica to a loading hook. Roger took Jessica's hand in his.

"That was a courageous rescue, even if it didn't work," Jessica said proudly.

"At least I'll die a brave rabbit," Roger said with a sigh.

"Enough!" Doom boomed, and he pulled another switch. Suddenly Roger and Jessica were hoisted high above the floor.

When Doom stepped back to make sure they were in range of the Dipmobile, he tripped on some stray Super-Smooth Gag Marbles. His feet slid out from under him, and he fell onto the floor with a thud. The weasels laughed so hard, they wound up rolling on the floor.

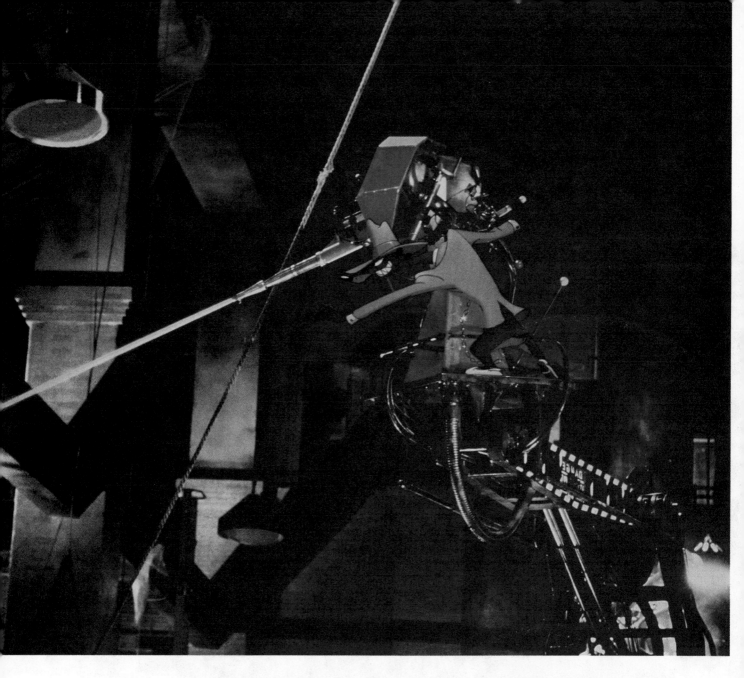

Judge Doom stood up slowly. His face looked so angry that the weasels instantly fell silent.

"Ready to fire, boss," said a weasel who was aiming a spray gun from atop the Dipmobile.

Doom turned to Eddie. "I hope you appreciate the fact that I am sparing your life long enough to see your Toon friends disappear forever in the Dip," Doom said with a sneer.

Eddie was surprised to feel tears welling up in his eyes. He had grown quite fond of the silly rabbit, and Jessica, too. All of Roger's joking and kidding could be annoying, but there was something very likable about the rabbit.

Just thinking about what made Roger so special gave Eddie an idea. In the silliest voice he began to sing a nutty song about his furry friend.

"Now, Roger is his name, laughter is his game..." Eddie sang as he duck-walked across the floor. The weasels started giggling.

"Don't be a dope, untie his rope, and watch him go insane..." Valiant went on dancing and goofing around as he'd seen Roger do at the Terminal Café. The weasels were now laughing wildly.

That gave Eddie a chance to grab some Delicious Dynamite Bombs. Eddie bit into one of the bombs. He spat out pieces that exploded at the feet of the laughing weasels and made them laugh even harder. Soon the weasels were helpless with laughter.

Eddie rushed for Doom, but he stopped in his tracks when the evil judge cracked open his cane to reveal a long gleaming blade. Eddie's eyes searched the Gag Factory for a weapon.

Eddie saw a huge magnet. He grabbed it and pointed it at Doom's sword. The sword flew out of Doom's hand with a clang. But then the magnet turned toward Eddie. It was being drawn by a large metal Ferris wheel behind him. The magnet pinned the detective to the Ferris wheel. Eddie struggled, but the magnet was too strong. Doom climbed onto a steamroller, and the engine roared to life. Doom headed straight for Eddie.

Roger and Jessica shut their eyes as they heard the steamroller chug toward Eddie. The detective looked down at the floor and saw a box of Portable Cartoon Holes. He reached down as far as he could and grabbed one of the holes. He slapped it over the magnet, and the magnet disappeared into the hole. Eddie jumped away just as the steamroller crashed into the Ferris wheel.

Valiant lunged at Doom and knocked him off the steamroller. Doom landed on his feet, ready to fight.

Roger and Jessica opened their eyes only to see Eddie and Doom about to be run over by the steamroller, which was spinning in circles with no one at the wheel. Eddie was desperate. He grabbed and threw the only thing he could reach—a can of Stay-Put Glue.

Valiant leapt out of the path of the steamroller, then watched in horror as Doom struggled to move. His feet were covered with the glue, and the steamroller was bearing down on him.

Eddie shuddered. Even an evil man like Doom didn't deserve such a terrible fate. But it was too late to help. The steamroller rolled right over Judge Doom. Eddie turned away.

"Eddie, look!" Roger shouted.

To Eddie's amazement there was Doom, flat as a pancake. Valiant watched as the edges of the pancake curled up and it wobbled off the floor.

Judge Doom staggered to a Gag Oxygen Tank and filled himself up with air. Suddenly Doom's hand was transformed into a buzz saw.

"You're—you're—" Eddie stammered.

"A Toon!" Doom hissed. "Yes. And the only one who'll be
left after I have my way."

Doom charged at Eddie with superhuman force. It seemed
as if Doom would overpower Eddie, but with his last bit of
strength Eddie managed to grab a Knockout Mallet.

Before Doom realized what was happening, Eddie pushed a
button, which sent a boxing glove on springs out of the mallet.
It hit the switch on the Dipmobile, whose spray gun was
pointing directly at Doom.

Dip gushed from the spray gun and covered Doom in a
stream of ink-dissolving chemicals. Roger and Jessica
shuddered as Doom melted like wax in a flame.

Doom was dissolved in his own Dip, and all of his evil schemes with him. Roger and Jessica sighed with relief, then thanked Eddie for saving them. Just then Dolores, Lieutenant Santino, and several other police officers burst into the factory.

"You could have a great future in show business," Roger told Eddie.

But Valiant wanted to stick to being a detective. "In fact, I'm not finished with this case yet," he said. "There are still a few loose ends I'd like to tie up."

"But, Eddie, you're hurt," Jessica observed.

"I am?" Eddie wondered. He looked down at his shirt and saw a dark stain.

"Marvin, that joker!" Valiant exclaimed.

Roger and Jessica didn't know what Eddie meant until he showed them a bottle of ink on Marvin's desk.

"Disappearing/Reappearing Ink," Roger announced.

Eddie snapped his fingers. "I've got it! Roger, where is that note you wrote in Jessica's dressing room the night all this started?"

Roger pulled the note from his pocket. Underneath Roger's note the words of Marvin's Last Will and Testament had returned in bold black and white:

"I, Marvin the Gag King, being of sound mind and body, do hereby leave the property known as Toontown to those lovable characters who have given me and the rest of humanity so much merriment and laughter...the Toons."

And that is how Toontown was saved by a brave rabbit and a silly detective.